Babbling Betty

Written by: **Mark McCraw**

Illustrated by: **Allison Vandenbosch**

This book is dedicated to all the babblers in the world.

My name is Betty. I have blonde hair and blue eyes. I am eleven years old. To see the board, I need to use big glasses even when I read books. I have one sister named Barbara, who has brown hair and blue eyes. Barbara is so beautiful. She was born before me. Barbara is twelve years old. My sister Barbara is shy, unlike me.

We both go to Burnham Elementary in Boston, Massachusetts. We live on 212 Baker Avenue in Bartonville, just outside of Boston. Our blue house has four bedrooms with three bathrooms. Next to our house is a brown barn.

My dad, Bob, is a banker. He is about five feet seven and has quite a belly. It is because he eats too much barbeque and too many biscuits. He works at Barton Bank in the downtown area of Boston. When he is at work, he likes to eat bagels. I think this is why he has a big bulging belly. At the bank, my dad gives out bubblegum to the kids. His favorite activity is watching baseball on the television after work. I am learning about the basics of baseball. My mom, Bianca, is about five feet four inches. She has blonde hair and blue eyes. She babysits children from the block.

On Saturdays, we eat barbeque at Brett's Barbeque Barn. It is a restaurant inside a barn. On Sundays. we go out to breakfast. Dad likes to order bacon and egg biscuits, but I prefer eggs and bacon with two slices of bread.

Mrs. Butler, my fourth-grade teacher, is a six-foot-tall lady. She has brown eyes and brown hair. She could be a basketball player because of her big stature. Both my best friends, Bobby and Brenda, have brown hair and blue eyes. Bobby and Brenda are shorter than I am.
People tell me I have a bad problem. I babble. I am a "babbler" at home, on the bus, and in class.

People describe me as a "brainiac" who babbles about baseball, butterflies, bowling, and books. I love to read books. At home, I babble to my young pugs, Brutus and Baxter. They were born to listen to me babble.

On the bus, I babble about all the books I have read. When I get to school, I babble in Mrs. Butler's class. My best friends are Bobby and Brenda, who sit in the back row next to me. They could not believe I had read so many books. I like to be a "blabber mouth" so the other classmates and Mrs. Butler hear me.

I like to babble about baseball, butterflies, bowling, and books. Mrs. Butler, Bobby, and Brenda are getting belligerent with me. They realize I am smart because I read so many books. Brenda and Bobby are getting bored with me. Brenda thinks I can also be bossy when I am not babbling. Because I was bothering Brenda and Bobby, Mrs. Butler moved me to near the blackboard next to her big desk.

I am sad about Bobby and Brenda. I thought they were my best buddies. I thought my babbling was fun. Sometimes, I feel like I do not belong. I felt betrayed by my best friends. I babbled under my breath at Mrs. Butler. I was not happy being at the blackboard because I did not think I was bad. I looked forward to leaving the school on the bus because I could babble more there than I could at the blackboard.

If the day could not get any stranger, we had two guest speakers, Benjamin and Betsy Hall. They told our class that a U.F.O. with aliens beamed them up to their spaceship. They said they saw blinking lights and a beeping sound up there. Betsy told us she knew it was not just a balloon. She and her husband said it was the biggest UFO ever. Benjamin said he first saw the aliens while driving his 1992 Brown Buick. The Halls claimed they were the only ones to have beamed up. After they beamed up, they said the aliens wiped their minds blank.

I did not believe the Halls' story, but my other classmates did believe them. I would have shaken in my boots if I saw an alien. They wanted the class to believe their weird story. I was not sure about believing them because their story was baffling. Being a babbler myself, I did not listen to their babbling. Other classmates believed them because they had seen it in alien books at the library.

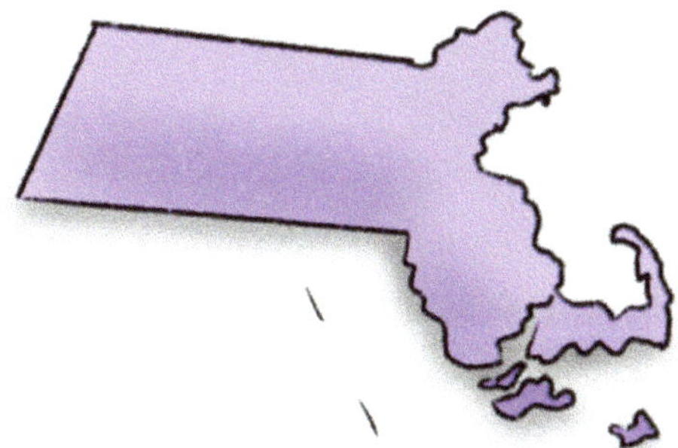

On the bus, I wondered why I got into trouble for babbling in class.
I was certain I could stop babbling again.
After thinking, I do not think I am mad at Bobby and Brenda
for being bored with my babbling. I could try and stop babbling.

One time, on a long and boring trip to Birmingham, Alabama, my dad became irritated by my babbling the whole time. My mother did not like my babbling either. My babbling was great until dad gave me the largest pack of bubblegum. I knew why my dad gave me bubblegum. It was to get me to stop babbling so much. So, on the trip, my dad stopped at Byrd's Gas Station.

My dad did not know I threw away the bubblegum in the bathroom. My dad had a battle plan for my constant babbling. He gave me his backup bubblegum pack that he keeps for babbling children in his back pocket. This was all because my babbling was bothering them.

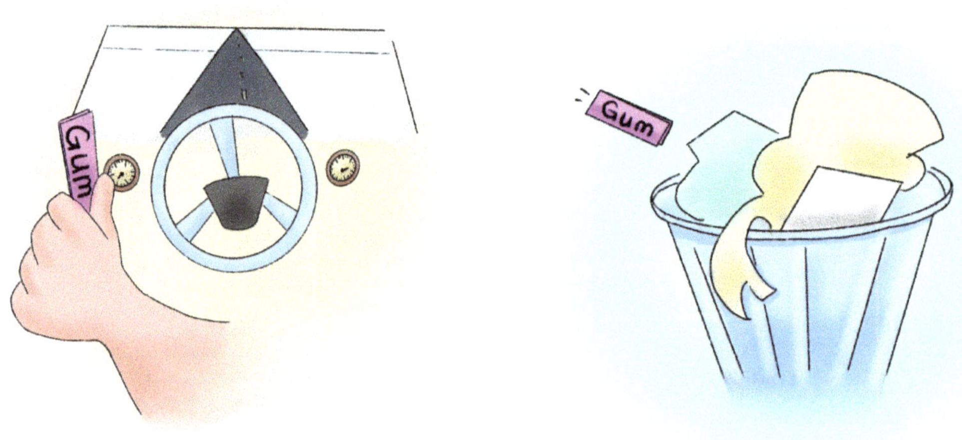

When we are at home, my mom and dad love it when I go to bed. They think it is a blessing when I am not babbling. I think I can still read books without babbling about them all the time. I have a "babbling" disease. They call me a "big mouth," but I know how brilliant I am because I read many books. I should stop babbling, or my best friends will not bare the babbling. Before my babbling becomes boisterous, I must write on the board, "I will not babble! I will not babble! I will not babble!"

Just when I thought I had my babbling under control, I met the boy of my dreams.

My classmate Ben was a new boy in class who wowed me. He just moved to Boston and enrolled in my classroom. He has dreamy brown hair and blue eyes. Now, I cannot stop babbling about him. He does not mind me babbling. Guess what! He is a known babbler too. He loves to talk about books and baseball.

Babblers cannot help themselves. Babbling is in our blood. I told Ben all about baseball, butterflies, bowling, and books. I even babbled about eating bacon and my dad eating biscuits. I talked about my dad having a big belly. I held nothing back with my big, blissful babbling. I had found my true beau.

Ben thought I was beautiful but wanted to be best buddies. This was not what I wanted. Oh well! Ben and I became Mrs. Butler's fourth-grade class's Best Babblers. We got a beautiful "Babbling" trophy. Ben and I are buddies because we love babbling. At least our classmates will never be bored!

My Babbles

My Babbles

My Babbles

My Babbles

My Babbles